Puffin Books
THE ELM STREET LOT

'Off to mischief, I suppose?' said surly Mr Cracken-thorpe.

'No,' said Sim Tolland, who was leading the Elm Street gang on that occasion, 'home to tea.' No need to mention that the dirt on their clothes and skin and hair had come from Mr Crackenthorpe's own roof-tiles, among others, and that only minutes before they had been descending the said roof-tiles on to his lean-to, and thence to his water-butt and the ground. Some things were better kept quiet, for the peace of mind of all.

Yet gimlet-eyed Mr Crackenthorpe might be forgiven for his suspicions, for that roof-top escapade was fairly typi-cal of the activities of the Elm Street children. When his handsome new bathtub was delivered to his home, wasn't it they who had invaded his front garden and rowed in the bath, pretending they were galley-slaves? And weren't they the ones who broke Miss Munson's front-room window, and released a hamster on the street, to the terror of all? Yes, there was no doubt about it, those children were an abomination, and whatever they did he'd put a stop to it, if he could!

Philippa Pearce was born and brought up in the Cambridgeshire village where she now lives. She spent many years in London and worked as a scriptwriter and producer in radio. These stories were written especially for the BBC TV programme *Jackanory*.

PHILIPPA PEARCE

The Elm Street Lot

ILLUSTRATED BY PETER RUSH

PUFFIN BOOKS

Puffin Books, Penguin Books Ltd, Harmondsworth, Middlesex, England
Viking Penguin Inc., 40 West 23rd Street, New York, New York 10010, U.S.A.
Penguin Books Australia Ltd, Ringwood, Victoria, Australia
Penguin Books Canada Limited, 2801 John Street, Markham, Ontario, Canada L3R 1B4
Penguin Books (N.Z.) Ltd, 182–190 Wairau Road, Auckland 10, New Zealand

First published by Kestrel Books 1979
Published in Puffin Books 1980
Reprinted 1981, 1983, 1984, 1985, 1987

These stories were first broadcast in a slightly different
form on BBC's *Jackanory* and published by the British Broadcasting
Corporation in 1969, with the exception of *Old Father Time*,
which was first published (under the title of *The Elm Street Lot and the Red
Sports Car*) in *Baker's Dozen*, edited by Leon Garfield (Ward Lock, 1974).

Printed and bound in Great Britain by
Cox & Wyman Ltd, Reading
Set in Monotype Baskerville

Contents

Mr Crackenthorpe's Bath

ELM STREET lies between Woodside School and the Park; and it really has an elm tree, or the remains of one. People that have lived a long time in Elm Street remember the tree: it was taller than any of the houses, they say, with branches from side to side of the street and green leaves all the summer through. The stump of this tree, standing at one end of the street, makes a perfect meeting-place for the Elm Street children – the Elm Street lot, as Woodside calls them. And at the other end of the street, looking straight down to the elm stump, lives gimlet-eyed old Mr Crackenthorpe.

'Cracky's coming!' call the Elm Street lot, scattering before him. They don't go round looking for trouble, of course, but sometimes it finds them. It found them when Mr Crackenthorpe's bath was delivered.

Not all the houses in Elm Street have baths, but the Council wants them everywhere. Mr Crackenthorpe hates the Council, and he said he'd make his own bathroom to please himself, thank you; and he bought a second-hand bath from heaven-knows-where.

It was delivered on the afternoon of a half-day at Woodside School, so the Elm Street lot were there to see it. It was the most splendid bath you could imagine, although the enamel inside was a bit worn, and there was some rust, too. The legs were the best part – huge-muscled legs like a dragon's, in scaly cast iron, with paws like a lion's, and claws into the bargain.

It was a particularly large bath – perhaps because Mrs Crackenthorpe is large. Mr Crackenthorpe had said he would get her into it and out again, even if it meant using a hoist.

The bath couldn't have been as heavy as it

looked: the lorry driver and his mate man-handled it off the lorry, and got it up to the Crackenthorpes' front door.

'Hooray and in she goes!' shouted Sim Tolland, who usually leads any cheering among the Elm Street lot. But the Crackenthorpes' front door is a bit narrow, and the bath was certainly wide. It wouldn't go through, in spite of the Elm Street lot's cheering, and the men's trying, and Mr Crackenthorpe's dancing about and shouting he'd have the law on everyone if the goods weren't delivered inside.

In the end the lorry driver and his mate dumped the bath in the Crackenthorpes' garden, which is just the size of an extra-wide bath. Only a low wall separates the garden from the pavement; so there the bath was, for all to see.

The Elm Street lot couldn't resist it. First of all,

Johnny and Kitty Bates got into it – at times when they knew that Mr Crackenthorpe was out doing the shopping. They pretended the bath was a boat, and rowed it with bits of stick and things. So many other children joined them that they became a whole crew of galley-slaves, rowing. Then it rained a bit, so that gave them the idea of pretending the galley was leaking dangerously and they baled out bilge-water with yoghurt cartons. And then Mr Crackenthorpe came home from the shops sooner than expected, and they all had to fly for their lives.

Mr Crackenthorpe stumped along to the Bateses' house to tell Mr Bates he must help him turn the bath upside down, so that his brats and the others couldn't go monkeying about with it. And Mr Bates told him to buzz off, or words to that effect.

So there the bath stood, outside the Crackenthorpes' front window, and there old Crackenthorpe mostly stood, too, on the other side of the
window, keeping watch. And meanwhile it rained

and it rained and it rained, and the bath filled up
steadily, until Bert Tolland, Sim Tolland's big
brother and rather a wit, said that the Crackenthorpes ought to apply to the Council to have the
horse-trough cleaned out. But, of course, the only
horse ever to go down Elm Street is the one that
draws the rag-and-bone-and-any-old-iron cart.
Unless you count the horse called Galloper, which
is really Jimmy Clegg. He is much too young to go
to Woodside School yet, and so horse-mad that he
makes little Maisie Padanah drive him up and
down Elm Street and will only talk to her in
whinnies.

By the time the weather cleared, the bath had filled right up with rainwater, and Miss Munson used to steal a drop after dark for her window-boxes. And at other times Johnny and Kitty Bates and Ginger Jones would sail paper boats in it, for dares. But then Mrs Clegg and Mrs Padanah started a song and dance about the water's being deep enough to drown one of the little ones; and suddenly all the mothers got bitter about the bath, and in the end Mr Clegg and Mr Padanah, with Bert Tolland, went to ask Mr Crackenthorpe to let them turn the bath upside down; and he said, 'Ho, Elm Street can change its mind, I see. And perhaps George Crackenthorpe has changed his mind, too!'

While old Crackenthorpe was enjoying himself being contrary, Mr Padanah said to the other two: 'What about it then?'

And Mr Clegg said: 'Right. Get a grip, Bert.'

And Bert said: 'Ready.'

Then the three of them took hold of that bath, and they managed to tilt it enough to empty some of the water out, and then to turn it over altogether, so that all the rainwater went over the

Crackenthorpes' front garden and then out through their front gate. Mr Crackenthorpe seemed almost to go out of his mind with rage. Bert and Mr Padanah and Mr Clegg followed the rainwater out, but Cracky went on dancing and shouting on top of his bath for a long time. The Elm Street lot watched him.

And then, three days later, the bath disappeared. It was there in the morning, when the Elm Street lot went to school. It was there at mid-day, when they came back for their dinners. And then, some time during that dinner-time, it vanished.

Of course, Mr Crackenthorpe said that the Elm Street lot had stolen it, which every one of them knew that they hadn't. And, as they said, they didn't care about him and his old bath and his threat to go to the police. But when they came out of school that afternoon and gathered at the tree stump as usual, old Mrs Crackenthorpe came waddling down the street to ask them – to *implore* them – to return the bath, as she put it. Her husband was down at the police station that very moment, she said – that was how she dared

to be doing what she was doing. And when the Elm Street lot said they'd had nothing to do with the bath's disappearance, she began to cry and said that Cracky was in such a carry-on she was sure he'd break a blood-vessel or have a seizure or do himself in somehow over it. And then she just went waddling back up the street, crying.

It was those tears – because Mrs Crackenthorpe is a nice old thing, really, and people feel sorry for her – that decided Sim Tolland. He drew the Elm Street lot round him and gave the order: 'Detect!'

The trouble was, there was just nothing for detectives to go on. All the Elm Street houses have their kitchens at the back, so that anyone at home was there, eating dinner, at the time the bath must have disappeared. The only exception seemed to be little Jimmy Clegg, who had got off his chair to run to the Cleggs' front-room window. When Sim asked him if he'd seen anything, he got scared and very muddled. His older sister, Vera, coaxed him; but all he said seemed to amount to this: he'd seen the Crackenthorpes' bath trotting down the street on its own four legs.

'*Clip, clop, clip, clop!*' said Jimmy Clegg, giving his usual imitation of a horse.

Jimmy's evidence sounded just little boy's imaginings; and there was only one other clue to go on – a roundish damp patch on the road outside the Crackenthorpes' house. Kitty Bates measured the patch with a tape – it was about eighteen inches across – and there seemed nothing more that could be done with it. Then Ginger Jones thought of getting down on his hands and knees to take a sniff. 'Phew!' he said, getting up again quickly. 'It's dung – or it *was* dung. Horse dung.'

The Elm Street lot were baffled. What horse – or horses? And who would have removed the horse-droppings so neatly, and why?

And then someone said: 'Miss Munson!' Little Miss Munson is a bit dotty about her gardening, and always on the look-out for compost or droppings of any kind to use as fertilizer. She's always ready, when the rag-and-bone cart comes round, to nip out with a shovel and collect any horse dung.

And then everyone realized where their detection had led them, for the rag-and-bone cart is also the any-old-iron cart.

The Elm Street lot tackled Miss Munson, who admitted that she'd heard horse's hooves and looked out. She'd seen horse-droppings, and at the same time seen the horse and cart, and the Crackenthorpes' bath driven off in it. She'd collected her droppings and kept her mouth shut, not wanting trouble. It looked as if Jimmy Clegg had heard what Miss Munson heard, and seen what she'd seen; but dressed it up a bit in his imagination. He's a very little boy.

That evening Sim Tolland got his big brother, Bert, to go with him at the head of the Elm Street lot, down to the junk-yard. Sim climbed up on Bert's shoulders to look over the wall into the yard, and there sure enough was the bath, looking as splendid as ever, with its paws in the air, like a contented dog. And there were the two rag-and-bone men sitting on a broken-down sofa, looking at the bath respectfully.

'Hi!' said Sim, over the wall; and the rag-and-bone men looked up and saw him, and one said quickly: 'This is private property.'

'The view's not private,' said Sim. 'Nice bath.'

'You get down and go home,' said the man. 'Quick.'

'What did he say?' asked Bert, partly because he really couldn't hear, with Sim trampling round his neck, and partly because he thought it was about time the rag-and-bone men knew that Sim wasn't perched up all by himself on stilts or something. Bert Tolland is a big young man, and his voice is big to match.

The rag-and-bone men asked Sim who he'd got on the other side of the yard wall.

'My big brother,' he said, 'and all the Elm Street lot.' And the Elm Street lot all stamped with their feet, to show they really were there. 'Nice bath,' Sim said again. 'Our Mr Crackenthorpe's lost a valuable bath like that. Down at the police station this minute, describing it for the C.I.D.'

'Go *on*,' said one rag-and-bone man; but the other one said, 'This isn't a valuable bath. In fact, it's a dead loss to us. Just takes up room. We're returning it to where we got it from.'

'No,' said the first rag-and-bone man.

'Yes,' said the second rag-and-bone man, who seemed a nervous man.

'Oh, all right, then,' said the first man, giving way. He stroked the bath's paws sadly.

'What do they say?' asked Bert.

'They're returning the bath,' said Sim; and at that the rest of the Elm Street lot stamped their feet in triumph. Someone happened to stamp on Bert Tolland's toe, and he yelped and tottered and he and Sim came down in a heap on the ground. No bones broken, but that was the end of the conversation over the wall.

Nobody ever knew for certain whether the rag-and-bone men really thought the bath had been put out for them, or whether they pinched it because they thought there was no one to see. Anyway, they must have panicked after Sim's

hint, for they came along that very night, really
late, and left the bath where they had found it.
At least, there it was next morning. Even Jimmy
Clegg hadn't heard horse's hooves this time.

Mr Crackenthorpe didn't like his bath mysteriously disappearing and appearing like that in
his own front garden, so he was civil enough when
Mr Clegg and Mr Padanah and Bert Tolland
came along and offered to take his front-room
sash window out and get the bath in that way.

So that was that. Bert Tolland must have said
something to Mrs Crackenthorpe, though, because
one day, when the coast was clear, she came down
to the stump and gave Sim Tolland a huge bag
of jelly babies for the Elm Street lot.

As far as anyone knows, Mr Crackenthorpe
never bought the hoist to get Mrs Crackenthorpe
in and out of the bath.

A Hamster at Large

IN the beginning there were no hamsters in Elm Street at all. Plenty of other pets, of course: dogs, cats, budgerigars, tortoises, and so on. Every one of the Elm Street lot had a pet, even if it was only Jimmy Clegg's caterpillar.

Everyone except Ginger Jones. It wasn't that the Joneses couldn't afford to keep an animal or bird of some kind – especially as Ginger was the only child, and his father had a good job on the railways, and his mother had always been a manager. Perhaps a bit too managing, people said. Even the dustbin men were frightened of her. She had a way of putting things, rather stately, and often sharp.

Ginger longed for a pet, but his mother always said the same thing: 'I have a husband and a son, both bringing dirt into the house and needing constant attention, day in, day out, week after week. I don't want another creature.' So no dog or cat or anything else for Ginger Jones.

'What about a hamster?' Sim Tolland had once said to Ginger. For although nobody in Elm Street owned a hamster, everyone knew they weren't much trouble, because Woodside School always has a hamster. It's part of their Nature.

Ginger shook his head hopelessly. 'Day in, day out,' he quoted, 'week after week, month after month, year after . . .'

Then Sim Tolland had his brain wave. You see, the Woodside hamster can never stay in the school in holiday-time – there's no one regularly to look after her. (This particular hamster was a female, called Elaine, after the school cook.) So, in holiday-time, one of the children – a different one each time – takes her home and looks after her until term starts again. Sim's brain wave was that Ginger Jones should take Elaine home.

His mother couldn't object to a *temporary* hamster; and the idea was that Elaine would give Mrs Jones a taste, so to speak, of hamsters. A nice taste, of course. She'd see what pretty, clean creatures they are. How little they eat. How little room a hamster's cage takes up; and so on.

Careful preparations were needed at Woodside. To begin with, every one of the Elm Street lot swore an oath not to offer, against Ginger, to take Elaine. As for children from other streets – they had to be persuaded to keep their mouths shut and their hands down when the teacher asked for a volunteer. You could offer them marbles or chewing-gum or iced lollies or peanuts, or you could offer to make them into mincemeat.

This part of the plan went well. At the end of term Miss Borwich said: 'Well, now, who wants Elaine this time?'

Absolute silence; absolute stillness. One or two of the children went pale with the strain; and somebody poked Ginger to wake him up. But he wasn't day-dreaming; just temporarily dazed. It had been arranged that he should speak up in a loud, clear, trustworthy voice; but all

that came out was a creaky whisper: 'Me. I'll take her.'

'No one else offering?' Miss Borwich said in surprise. She looked round at everybody, and everybody stared back at her, willing her to hand Elaine over to Ginger. She looked at Ginger, and he managed a trustworthy smile.

'Well,' Miss Borwich said uneasily, 'if Herbert Jones is the only one to volunteer—'

'He is,' said Sim Tolland.

'Then he must take Elaine. I'm sure Herbert will take great care of her.' Ginger nodded as if his head were coming loose. 'And you others,' Miss Borwich said sternly, 'I hope this doesn't mean you're losing your interest in Nature.'

'Oh, no, Miss Borwich!' everyone said gratefully.

So Ginger took Elaine home.

Now Elaine really was a beauty – Ginger said she could have been a beauty queen. She was nearly as big as half a pound of butter, and in parts not far off the same colour. She had bright little black eyes – only Mrs Jones called them beady – and she had a nice character. Quite soon Ginger taught her to run up his arm on to his shoulder and then, standing on her hind legs, to reach for some favourite food – a sunflower seed or a cornflake – which he had lodged behind his ear. There was a little exercise-wheel in Elaine's cage, and every evening she would get on to it and pedal it round: *creak! creak! creak!* Mr Jones said the sound got on his nerves. He called the wheel her treadmill, although no one *made* Elaine go on it, of course. Mr Jones wasn't really a nervy man by nature; but he'd been a prisoner of war in the last war, and he said that when he saw Elaine standing on her hind feet up at the bars, it gave him a funny feeling.

Partly because of that, partly because he'd have done anything for Elaine, Ginger decided to make her a bigger, grander cage than the school one. He knew what he was doing, and the new cage, when it was finished, was fit for a princess, with all kinds of little improvements. One thing turned out to be not an improvement: Ginger backed the cage with wood, without any wire-mesh reinforcement. Soft wood, too; and in the night Elaine gnawed a hole right through it and escaped. Disappeared.

Ginger was very much upset, and so was his mother. Ginger thought that Elaine might starve; and Mrs Jones said, on the contrary, she couldn't bear the idea of that hamster running loose in the house and *fingering* everything eatable. She also said she lay awake at night hearing Elaine climbing up the legs of the bed.

Ginger's father said nothing, but he wouldn't help to look for Elaine.

That Sunday morning, early, there was a commotion from the house next door to the Joneses', where the Cleggs live. The Cleggs' front door was flung open and Mrs Clegg rushed out into the street. She was holding an opened cornflake packet in her hand, and she seemed to be shaking the packet wildly, and screaming. It was just as if she were getting an electric shock from the packet, but couldn't break the contact and get rid of the thing. It turned out that the corn-flake packet was being shaken *from the inside*; not by Mrs Clegg at all. When Mrs Clegg re-covered enough presence of mind to throw the packet from her, skimming it along the street, out popped Elaine. Out she popped, and under Sim

Tolland's big brother's second-hand car, covered with plastic sheeting.

With Mrs Clegg having hysterics in the middle of Elm Street, everyone got to know what was going on. In a matter of seconds Ginger Jones and the rest of the Elm Street lot were on their hands and knees, peering under the car.

'I can see her!' said Ginger.

'If you mean that yellowish thing,' said Sim Tolland, 'it looks more like an old banana skin to me.'

'I'd know her anywhere,' said Ginger. 'It's her.'

'Whatever it is,' said someone else, 'it's not moving.'

'She's petrified with fright,' said Ginger. 'We shall have to move the car to get her.'

They had to move Mrs Clegg first, who was still laughing and sobbing about the packet of cornflakes. Then, having got the car key, they opened the door, took off the brake, and pushed the car out of its old position. All that time Ginger was on his stomach, watching the yellowish blur, saying, no, she wasn't moving, and he only hoped she hadn't died of fright.

When they'd got the car away, they found that the yellowish blur was an old curled up banana skin; and they noticed a kind of over-hang to the kerb of the pavement there, and Elaine must have run along under that – right away, and heaven knew where she was now.

For several days there was no sign whatsoever of Elaine. (It turned out later that she must have wandered away into one of the other streets whose gardens or yards back on to Elm Street.) Ginger was very low-spirited indeed. He said that he knew in his bones that one of the Elm Street cats had mistaken Elaine for a mouse, and eaten her.

Then, after several days, people in Elm Street began to complain of odd noises that might be rats or mice, but weren't; hamster-hoards of food were found.

Elaine was back.

Hamsters like travelling, especially by tunnel, and it can't have been too difficult in the terrace houses of Elm Street, especially with lofts whose partition walls are old and sometimes in bad condition. Elaine was seen only twice in the next few weeks. Once was by old Mr Crackenthorpe, when he was attending to the water-tank in his roof. He saw her and shouted at her: 'You get out, or I'll boil you for my tea!' Elaine did get out.

And then Ginger saw her. He was at the elm stump by himself and very melancholy. Everyone else had gone off to the Park, but he simply hadn't the heart for it. The sparrows were pecking about as usual, because the Elm Street lot often pass round, say, biscuits or peanuts, and then there are crumbs. Today someone had spilt some pop-corn.

It was very quiet, and Ginger was leaning sadly against the stump without moving. And then, with his downcast eyes, he saw Elaine – saw her come creeping out of the tree stump itself, between his very feet. He held his breath and watched her; she collected several of the pieces of popcorn in her cheek pouches and then slipped back by the way she had come.

He stooped to examine the bottom of the tree stump. There was a hole that must be Elaine's front-doorway. It was big enough for Ginger to get two fingers in – and then Elaine bit them. But they had been in long enough to touch more than Elaine: she had babies with her. That's why it's certain that she had spent some time out of Elm Street, where there were no other hamsters, and somewhere else met a male hamster also on the run, and mated with him.

Now she had babies – there were nine of them. Ginger, with Sim Tolland, managed to get the whole family out of the stump and back into the old cage. The cage was then kept in the Tollands' house. When the babies were old enough, Ginger and Sim gave them away, up and down Elm Street, and what with those hamsters and their descendants, there are always hamsters in Elm Street nowadays.

As for Elaine, Ginger took her back to Woodside at the end of the holidays. Miss Borwich, when she heard about the babies, said that she hoped the experience would be a warning to Elaine.

And Ginger? It would have been nice to have ended the story with Ginger's mother welcoming one of Elaine's babies into their home; but Mrs Jones said another hamster would enter the house only over her dead body.

So Ginger would have ended as he began, without a pet, if it hadn't been for the burglary.

Burglars broke into the Joneses' house one Saturday afternoon when everyone was out. They didn't take anything much, but they made a mess of everything, and Mrs Jones was very, very much upset: she washed everything in the house that was washable, and disinfected everything else. She put a notice on the gate saying, 'Beware of the dog', and she hung a dog's lead and muzzle in the hall, where anyone could see who looked through the letter-box. She even kept a bowl of water in sight there, with DOG written round the bowl. Still she didn't feel safe, so, in the end, without telling Ginger – it was the biggest and best surprise of his life – she made Mr Jones buy a dog. Biter (that was what Mrs Jones said the dog must be called) was huge, with the wolfish look of an Alsatian and the bay of a bloodhound. His nature was timid but affectionate. He loved Ginger, and Ginger loved him: Biter was Ginger's dog.

Rooftop

IN a really rainy season there's always some family in Elm Street whose roof begins to leak. The last time, it was the Tollands'.

Mrs Tolland had discovered the leak, in three separate places, through the skylight over the stairs. She'd put three saucepans on three separate stairs to catch the drips, which they were doing. She'd also just persuaded Mr Tolland, who was off work with a very heavy cold, that he'd better go up to bed after all. He'd started slowly upstairs, when Sim began coming down. He came down fast, two at a time, as is the custom with most of the Elm Street lot, and he didn't take full account of the saucepans on the stairs. He kicked the top one by mistake, and that bounced down on to the middle one, which bounced down on to the bottom one, and all three bounced their water over Mr Tolland as he was coming up. With surprising speed for someone with a highish temperature – but he was very much annoyed – Mr Tolland tried to box Sim's ears as he shot by, but missed and hit one of the saucepans into the hall mirror and shattered it. Then Mrs Tolland, at the foot of the stairs, burst into tears.

As Sim Tolland said, it was a very good beginning for seven years of bad luck. He mopped up the stairs and his father as best he could, and put the saucepans back into position, and brushed up the broken looking-glass, and went to fetch old Mr Friday. Old Mr Friday used to be a builder; but he's retired from all that – except for the roof-work. Roofs have always been his passion.

With his mac over his head, Sim tore through rain and wind to the Fridays' house. Young Mrs Friday opened the door, and Sim explained about the leaks.

'Grandad!' young Mrs Friday shouted into the house, and some more shouting brought old Mr Friday shuffling to the front door.

'Well,' said Mr Friday to Sim, 'whose roof?'

'Ours. Tolland. Number Twenty-two.'

'Wait a minute,' said Mr Friday. He went back down the hall to the coat-pegs. He took from them the clothes without which he was never seen out of doors in Elm Street: a flat cap, fawn-coloured, and an old fawn raincoat. Wearing these, he went out as far as the Friday's front gate to look up at the sky, from which the rain was still emptying itself without ceasing. 'That'll stop within the hour,' Mr Friday said. 'Then I'll come.'

Sim Tolland went home with the message.

Forty minutes later the rain had stopped, all but a few drops carried on gusty winds. In cap and raincoat old Mr Friday made his way slowly down Elm Street, carrying his long ladder; and at the same time the first of the Elm Street lot came out to see anything that was to be seen. They collected at the Tollands' front gate, because that was where old Mr Friday was going to set up his ladder. Sim had passed the word around.

Mr Friday set his ladder up with its foot just inside the front gate and its top resting against the parapet of the roof. He slowly mounted it, hoisted himself skilfully over the parapet, and moved out of sight towards the back of the house. Then he appeared again, spreadeagled against the slates of the roof, examining them with loving interest.

While he was still aloft, Mrs Tolland came out to see how things were going. She could not see Mr Friday, so she called up to him; but Mr Friday did not hear her. Then Sim Tolland and the rest of the Elm Street lot shouted as loudly as they could 'MR FRIDAY!' and he came to the parapet and craned his head over.

'Have you found what's wrong?' called Mrs Tolland.

Well, said Mr Friday cautiously, there were three places where it was possible that rain might have been coming through. He seemed about to add more, when Mrs Tolland went indoors again rather suddenly, slamming the front door behind her. Either the vibration of the slam or the nearly upside-down position of Mr Friday's head – or the two things together –

caused the accident: Mr Friday's flat cap fell off his head with a kind of downward swoop that carried it over the Tollands' front fencing and – with a gust of wind still helping – into a deep puddle. There, before the horrified gaze of the Elm Street lot, the cap filled with water and sank to the bottom.

Mr Friday came down the ladder as quickly as he could, and when he reached the bottom Sim Tolland was holding his cap out to him, only it looked more like a floor cloth in use than a flat cap. Nobody could have worn it. Mr Friday fingered the sodden cap in a very upset way, flustered. He had meant to take the ladder down and carry it home, and have some tea, and a rest, and come back with the ladder and his tools after tea – or possibly the next morning. Now, with no cap on his head, he felt all at sixes and sevens.

He wondered what to do; he hesitated; he made up his mind – and he unmade it. At last, in desperation, holding the cap with care in both hands, he set off for home. He would get the cap business settled first; then deal with the ladder. As he was going, he remembered the

Elm Street lot, still standing sympathetically near. 'Mind,' he said, 'no touching that ladder. I'll be back.'

Probably the Elm Street lot would have had the idea of climbing Mr Friday's ladder sooner or later, anyway, but his saying that gave them the idea at once. Sim Tolland was the first to go up, of course, since it was his roof. He went up and over the parapet and out of sight. Kitty and Johnny Bates went next; then Ginger Jones. Two more were on the ladder, and all the Elm Street lot might have ended up on the Tollands' roof; but now, down the street, the Crackenthorpes' front door opened and Mr Crackenthorpe came out to do the shopping as usual.

Mr Crackenthorpe saw the group at the foot of the ladder, and the two climbing up it. The

four already on the roof had dodged below parapet-level.

'Hi!' shouted Mr Crackenthorpe, and started down the street. At once the two on the ladder scrambled down, and the whole lot began to run. 'Wait!' shouted Mr Crackenthorpe, but nobody did.

Mr Crackenthorpe went down the street to the Tollands' house, knocked at the door, and asked Mrs Tolland if she realized that half the Elm Street lot were trying to break their necks on old Friday's ladder left outside her house. He said a good deal more, loudly; and Mr Tolland from his bed, heard him. Suddenly, from the top of the stairs now, he joined in, calling to his wife that she could tell old Crackenthorpe from him that he could –

At this point Mrs Tolland slammed the door for the second time that day.

The four on the roof hadn't been able to see any of this, of course, but they had heard it all; and now they could see old Mr Friday in the distance, coming back to fetch his ladder. He was wearing the bowler he reserved for weddings and funerals. It felt very unfamiliar, and his nerves were on edge.

Mr Crackenthorpe was lying in wait for Mr Friday, by Mr Friday's ladder.

Now these two old men had known each other all their lives: one of them had been born in Elm Street; the other just round the corner. They had been at Woodside School together, in the old days, long before Miss Borwich. They'd grown up together; and they'd never, never got on.

'Well, Old Man Friday!' said Mr Crackenthorpe; and Mr Friday's face clouded over.

'Ah!' said Mr Friday.

'What about this ladder?' said Mr Cracken-thorpe.

'What ladder?' said Mr Friday, as though Mr Crackenthorpe were seeing things.

'This ladder!' said Mr Crackenthorpe, shaking it so suddenly and violently that Sim Tolland and the others, hidden aloft near the ladder's top, nearly jumped out of their skins.

'You mean *my* ladder?' said Mr Friday.

'What's it doing here?'

'I have erected it to inspect the roof,' said Mr Friday.

'But what's it doing here by itself, with nothing to stop all the kids of Elm Street from climbing it and breaking their necks?'

'What's it doing here by itself?'

'That's what I said.'

There was a pause, while the four on the roof wondered what the two below were doing. Nothing, perhaps; just glaring at each other.

Then: 'George Crackenthorpe,' Mr Friday said at last, 'I'll trouble you not to waste my precious time with your conversation. I've come to fetch my ladder home.' And from the sound

of it, he was taking the ladder down; and Mr
Crackenthorpe was making no objection to that,
but concentrating on what Mr Friday had referred
to as his conversation. He finished up by calling
after Mr Friday: 'Somebody should put a stop
to you, Old Man Friday!'

'Ah!' said Mr Friday.

Mr Friday went off with his ladder, and Mr
Crackenthorpe went off, growling, to his shopping; and the four on the roof were left to the
problem of reaching ground-level again with no
ladder to help them. With nobody to help them,
either, for – with the best will in the world – the
rest of the Elm Street lot were powerless.

On the roof, Sim Tolland took charge. 'The

front's no good to us,' he said. 'The drop to the pavement is too sharp.'

'Drop?' said Johnny Bates, peering over the parapet: his face went greenish. Kitty held his arm.

Ginger said, 'What's the idea then, Sim?'

'The back. Come on,' said Sim; and they moved cautiously, in single file, to the back of the Tollands' house. They were now over-looking the Tollands' little garden, but with no means of getting into it. However, it was possible, because of the terracing of the houses, to move easily from roof to roof, and there were some roofs from which a good climber could descend. Low outhouses and lean-tos had been added to the main buildings over the years, and sometimes these made a kind of rough stairway down to the ground level of back garden or back yard.

To choose from, there was Miss Munson's back garden, the Joneses' back yard, the Cracken-thorpes' back yard, –

'That's it!' Sim cried suddenly. 'Old Cracky's out shopping – we know that. That gives us just half an hour, say.'

'What about Mrs Cracky?'

'Pooh!' said Sim; and they trusted him.

So, still in single file, they began to move from roof to roof, very carefully. They would have liked to dawdle and explore as they went,

but they knew that time was against them. Even so, between them, they made some interesting finds: several birds' nests, of course; three balls, one of them in good condition; the skeleton of a kite, very old; an empty beer bottle; an Edward VII shilling; and a rusty metal object which Kitty Bates said was a cheese grater.

They reached the Crackenthorpes' roof. Sim, alone, slid from the roof of the house on to the roof of Mr Crackenthorpe's lean-to and thence on to his water-butt and thence to the ground. At once he went to the door that led from the garden into the house. They heard him knock loudly; they heard Mrs Crackenthorpe come to open the door, with exclamations of amazement. Then they heard Sim beginning some very long and soothing explanation. At the end of it Mrs Crackenthorpe was laughing wheezily; and Sim called to the other three: 'Come on!'

They never knew quite how Sim had squared Mrs Crackenthorpe. But, anyway, unlike her husband, she had rather a soft spot for the Elm Street lot, particularly Sim Tolland. So the four of them walked through the Crackenthorpes' house, out through the front door – Mrs Cracken-thorpe, still laughing to herself, closing it promptly and softly behind them – and out through the front gate and on to the pavement. As they stood there, breathing in liberty, Mr Crackenthorpe came round the corner into Elm Street, his shopping done. He looked at them suspiciously. They had a good deal of roof dirt on their clothes and skin and hair, and were carrying the three balls, the beer bottle, the cheese grater, and the rest.

'Off to mischief, I suppose?' said Mr Crackenthorpe.

'No,' said Sim Tolland truthfully, 'home to tea.'

Old Father Time

THE Elm Street lot like to hang together: there may be arguments round the old tree stump, but not often quarrelling. Never – or almost never – fighting.

The last time there was a fight, it was between Sim Tolland and Johnny Bates; and it was about the peace and quiet of Elm Street. Elm Street usually *is* very quiet, especially in the evening; but Di Bates and Old Father Time made two exceptions to that.

Di Bates, whose full name is Diana Marilyn Bates, is a lot older than Johnny and Kitty, and the prettiest girl in Elm Street and for miles round. She's always being taken out in the evening, to dances and cinemas and for moonlight walks. At first it was Sim Tolland's big brother,

Bert, who took her; and that was peaceful for everybody. They'd stroll back in the evening to Elm Street from wherever it was; Bert would see Di to her front-door; then he'd walk on to his own.

But Di threw Bert Tolland over for a boy with a motorbike and – Di riding pillion – they'd come roaring back late in the evening from wherever it was, and then the bike would go roaring off again. Then just when poor Bert Tolland had saved up to buy an old second-hand car, Di Bates threw the motorcyclist over for a boy with a smart red sports car, and they'd come roaring back from wherever it was, and there'd be a lot of door slamming at midnight before Red Sports Car roared off again. Altogether Di Bates's boy-friends were a trial to the sleepers of Elm Street.

And then there was the Tollands' cat. Perhaps once, long ago, he had been a kitten, called Fluffy or Tibs or something like that; but now he was just called Old Father Time. He was old, old; and he had lost an eye, and limped badly. And Old Father Time's habit every so often was to saunter slowly down Elm Street at about midnight, yowling.

The night before the fight at the tree stump, Old Father Time was doing this as usual, and Mr Crackenthorpe had troubled to get out of bed and open a front window and throw a boot – with shocking aim. He had hit a street lamp, breaking the glass. All that he had then said about Old Father Time had been overheard quite clearly by Mrs Bates, who was sitting up in bed waiting for Di to get home. And she had told most of it to Mr Bates, over breakfast, and so Johnny and Kitty Bates knew it and could tell the rest of the Elm Street lot later, round the tree stump.

Kitty Bates said: 'Old Cracky finished up by shouting at the top of his voice that that diseased old rag-bag of a tom-cat should be put down.'

'And if your dad wouldn't do it, Sim,' said Johnny Bates, 'then old Cracky himself would go round to the animal cruelty people and ask them to do it.'

Sim Tolland was annoyed. 'Perhaps you don't know what my dad said to old Cracky when he came puffing round this morning?'

'Go on,' said Johnny.

'He said that if anyone needed putting down

it was old Cracky, and he'd ask the Council to do it, and to send the Refuse Disposal to clear up afterwards.'

Everyone at the tree stump liked that; but Sim wasn't content, perhaps because he knew – and he knew that Johnny Bates knew – about Bert's being thrown over by Di. He went on: 'And then my dad said that if Cracky really objected to noise at night, why hadn't he the guts to throw his other boot at that red sports car with no silencer that brings your sister home every night; and give up persecuting poor old defenceless cats?'

'Who says that sports car hasn't a silencer?' said Johnny.

'I do,' said Sim.

But, of course, they weren't quarrelling about a car-silencer. The next remark brought them a bit nearer to what they *were* quarrelling about.

'Anyway,' said Johnny, 'that sports car really goes, which is more than can be said for your brother's poor old second hand thing living under its plastic sheet.'

That was when Sim Tolland went for Johnny Bates, and Johnny Bates fought back.

You might have thought the fight would have been over in half a minute or so, because Sim is older and bigger and stronger than Johnny; but it wasn't, and that was because of Kitty Bates. She'd been standing by, listening, with the rest of the Elm Street lot, and now she went right in to help Johnny, fighting like a demon. She's tough. Sim Tolland – who rather likes her in peacetime – held her right off the ground by her hair, but she just went on biting.

Nobody knows who might have won, because just then Bert Tolland himself turned up, on his way home. Kitty Bates drew off at once; and Bert took a good hold of the other two and pulled them apart to stop them. Then he saw who they were.

'My!' he said, good tempered, if gloomy. 'My, my! I thought you two were always as thick as thieves – and up to as much good. What's made you fall out now? What's up?'

At first neither of them wanted to say, but Bert gave them both a bit of a shake, and then Sim said: 'He was saying things about Old Father Time.'

Bert Tolland laughed; and that annoyed both Sim and Johnny.

Johnny said quickly, 'And *he* was saying things about the sports car that brings Di home.'

Bert Tolland stopped laughing, and frowned.

Sim went on eagerly, 'And *he* said the sports car was better than your car; and *I* was saying –'

Bert Tolland never heard what Sim had said.

He was scowling ferociously, and he shook those two boys until the rest of the Elm Street lot heard their teeth clattering in their heads. Then he took Johnny Bates by the scruff of his collar, like a puppy, and set him on the top of the Elm Street stump; and he took Sim also by the scruff and pushed him ahead of him to the Tollands' house and in through the front door, and then the front door slammed behind them both. And what Bert Tolland said to Sim Tolland on the other side of that door, nobody knows.

And that was the end of the fighting, but not of the story.

That night Red Sports Car brought Di Bates home as usual, and that night, as usual, Old Father Time decided to take his stroll down Elm Street. And as Red Sports Car was roaring off again from the Bateses' house, it met Old Father Time in the middle of the street; the car screeched its brakes for as long as it takes to run over and kill a cat, and then it roared on and away, and there was poor Old Father Time lying dead in the middle of the road.

People didn't rush out of their houses at the

noise, as they would have done in the daytime. But two people in Elm Street, in two different houses, had been listening particularly for the sound of the red sports car: one of them was Di Bates, of course, just home, still dressed up from her evening out; and the other was Bert Tolland, insomniac.

Within half a minute of the screeching of brakes Di Bates had reopened their front door to see what had happened, and within another half minute Bert Tolland was peering out, too. What he saw was Di Bates now standing in the middle of Elm Street, looking down – he couldn't see what she was looking at – and something about the way she stood there made him want to rush out to her. But it was weeks since Di Bates and Bert Tolland had as much as said good-day to each other; so Bert Tolland rushed back into the house and up to Sim's room and began pulling him

out of bed and putting shoes on him and a coat round him.

'What – what on earth is it?' said Sim sleepily.

'Shut up – shut up! Get up and get out into the street and ask Di what's the matter. And if anything is the matter, call me and I'll come.'

Sim was now wide awake, but just as confused as if he weren't.

'But, Bert – ' he began.

'Do me this favour,' said Bert, 'and I'll do anything for you – anything. Go and make sure that Di Bates is all right; and I'll give you the moon. I promise.'

Bert's promise somehow cleared Sim's head; but he wanted to be quite sure. 'Suppose I wanted to go with you in the first real trip in the car?'

'Yes, yes.'

'And me, not you, to decide which is the first real trip?'

'Yes, yes, *yes*. Only *go*.'

So Sim went, bouncing out of the house for joy at the thought of Bert's promise. And there was Di Bates still in the middle of Elm Street, but kneeling now, and when Sim saw what she was kneeling by – poor Old Father Time's body – all the bounce went out of Sim.

'Oh!' he said. He stood still as a statue of

marble. Bert Tolland, peering through the crack of their front door, saw Di Bates get up and put her arm round him.

'He must have been killed at once,' Di said to Sim. 'The car must have gone right over him.'

'He never even stopped,' said Sim. He meant the driver, whose name you will not be told, for a reason that comes later.

'He can't have realized what he'd done,' said Di.

Sim moved. He began to stoop: 'I'll take him.'

'Just a minute.' Di stripped off a smart new cardigan, and they wrapped Old Father Time in it. Then Sim carried him back to the Tollands' house, where Bert met him at the door, and Bert carried the bundle into the back garden, where Old Father Time had often taken the sun or a sparrow, as the case might be.

Then and there, by moonlight, they buried him,

so that their mother would not see him in the morning – although she and Mr Bates would have to be told, of course. They did not bury him in Di's cardigan, but Sim fetched a piece of clean sacking, and Bert dug a hole three spits deep, and so they buried him; and later in the year Sim planted forget-me-nots over him.

The next morning Sim, pale from grieving and lack of sleep, told their parents. Mrs Tolland was terribly upset, and cried, as had been expected. Mr Tolland, to comfort her and Sim said that, after all, Old Father Time had been getting on: he was bound to go some day.

'But not run over by a car,' said Sim.

'By a car that didn't trouble to stop,' said Bert.

'I expect that young fellow of Di Bates's didn't realize,' said Mr Tolland.

'Didn't realize – nothing!' said Bert.

When she felt better, Mrs Tolland washed Di's cardigan and was going to take it back to her when Bert said: 'I'll take it – this evening.'

By that evening, of course, the whole of Elm Street had heard of the death, and a good many were wondering what was going to happen next. In spite of the lateness of the hour, there were quite a few of the Elm Street lot gathered at the tree stump to see the red sports car come as usual to pick Di Bates up. Sim was all for tackling the driver at once, but Bert said, 'Wait.'

He came. He drove his red sports car with the

usual roar and rattle up to the Bateses' house, and at once the front door opened and there was Di Bates, all dressed up for the dance they were going to.

'Hello!' said Red Sports Car. 'Ready?'

'Yes.' But she hesitated. 'Last night, when you were driving away, the car hit something.'

'Hit something?'

'A cat.'

'Did it?'

'Didn't you know?'

'Well, now you mention it . . . In fact, I thought I'd probably killed the thing.'

Di stared for a long minute, and then – like Bert Tolland earlier – she said, 'Wait.'

She went indoors and came out again with her mother's shopping basket. From this she began to take a number of things in a hurry: a little bottle of scent, a box of scented soap, an embroidered handkerchief, bathsalts – all the things that Red Sports Car had ever given her. One by one, but quite fast, she threw them at him or on the ground near him. There were even two bunches of wet-stemmed flowers and a box of chocolates, half eaten. The Elm Street lot crawled over the ground afterwards and collected everything of use, so they knew.

At the very end, so that there could be no mistake, Di Bates slapped his face. Then she went indoors, and Red Sports Car called some names after her and then drove off at a really frightful speed, still shouting. And this is why it wasn't worth telling you his proper name, for he was never, never seen in Elm Street again.

That was the moment that Bert Tolland chose for the returning of Di Bates's cardigan. Mrs Bates, who answered the door to him, said that Di was really in no fit state to see anybody; but Bert just sidled in, and Mrs Bates had to shut the door behind him, and that was that.

For the rest of that week Di Bates didn't go out in the evening at all; but Bert Tolland became cheerful again. He took the plastic cover off his old car and began tinkering with it to make it go properly. He wanted it right for an afternoon trip on Saturday, he said.

'Where to?' Sim asked.

'Right into the country,' Bert said blithely. 'Di says she'll come. To Borden Woods and then to Borden Bridge, where you can hire a boat.'

'I'll come too,' said Sim.

'You're joking,' said Bert, grinning. Then he stopped grinning, as he remembered his midnight promise: 'No, you're not.'

Sim wasn't joking. He was choosing to go on this first long car trip, when Bert happened to be taking Di. Nothing Bert could say would budge him.

Bert was very upset; but Di Bates – for a wonder – was not. She laughed a lot, and said that if Sim were coming, then it would be just as well if Kitty and Johnny came too. So they all went.

Saturday was fine, and the old car went like a bird. They got to Borden Woods, but not to the

64

river. In the woods Kitty and Johnny and Sim stuck together, but they got separated from the other two, somehow. They were looking for each other, on and off, for hours on end.

When at last they did find each other, it was time to go home. Bert and Di were not as cross as might have been expected. Bert said he had enjoyed the afternoon, in spite of everything; and Di Bates laughed a lot.

Kite-crazy

THERE are plenty of times, even out of school-hours, when the tree stump is deserted. The Elm Street lot has gone elsewhere, usually to the Park.

The Park is the name the Council has given to what used to be wasteland and trees. The Council has laid out one part as a playground with swings and a monster sand-pit. There is also a cafeteria, and asphalted paths, and the Council lops the trees. But beyond this part the ground begins to rise, buildings and trees are left behind, and you reach what everybody – everybody except the Council – has always called Old Baldhead, or Old Baldie. Old Baldhead is just a hill or hillock, bald of trees, but grassy; it's the highest point for some miles around, and the most open and windy.

This is where the Elm Street lot go kite-flying, when the craze is on them.

Up the hill they go: Sim Tolland in the lead,

because somehow he usually does lead; and he is carrying the kite. Then, close behind, with an anxious eye on the kite, Ginger Jones, who made it. Then Kitty and Johnny Bates and the rest of the Elm Street lot; and Vera Clegg. Vera Clegg always comes last and far behind, because she has her little brother, Jimmy, in his pushchair – his horse-box, he calls it. Sometimes Maisie Padanah comes too, squashed in on top of Jimmy. That makes Vera Clegg even slower up the hill.

By the time Vera reaches the top of Old Baldie, the Elm Street lot has probably managed to get the kite up.

'There she goes!' Sim Tolland says softly, over and over again, as he lets the kite-string out. And there she goes – up and up, higher and higher, smaller and smaller in the distances of the sky, until you can't believe the kite-string stretches right up there, because it's become invisible; and if you look away and then look back, you can't believe there's a kite there either, until you search the sky with your eyes. Then you see her, sitting high up there as easily as one of the Elm Street lot might sit on a brick wall.

Once the kite's right up, anyone can have a turn at holding the string; and – if anyone has remembered to bring some paper – messengers can be sent up to it. A messenger is just a bit of paper – any old bit – that's slotted on to the kite-string at the bottom; and then, steadily, as if by magic, it will rise up the kite-string – up – up – up – until it can go no farther; until it reaches the kite itself, in fact.

There was a time when Sim Tolland wrote things – rude things – on his messengers before sending them up. That was for a kite they called Miss Borwich. At that time Sim was not getting on too well with the real Miss Borwich at Woodside School. So he took Ginger's new kite and painted Miss Borwich's face on it – at least, he said it was that, although it didn't look much like a face at all. The kite called Miss Borwich soothed Sim Tolland. He liked seeing her go up and away – away into the farthest distance; and then he liked sending his special messengers up to her there. It made him feel better, he said.

One day, perhaps because he was thinking of

the kite as Miss Borwich, he had trouble in bringing her safely down again.

'You want to look out for those tree-tops,' said Ginger Jones. 'She's beginning to swoop a bit.'

'Oooh!' said Vera Clegg, her hand up to her mouth; and Kitty and Johnny Bates stopped messing about on the slopes of Old Baldie to stare, too.

'She's all right,' said Sim.

Ginger mentioned that this was the best kite he'd made so far.

'All right, then,' said Sim. 'Bring her down yourself!' But at that moment, with a swoop more sudden than anything ever managed by the real Miss Borwich in a Woodside classroom, the kite flung itself headlong into the top of one of the trees

on the lower slopes of Old Baldie, and settled there.

'Now look what you've done!' said Ginger.

'Keep your bright hair on,' said Sim. 'She's not spoilt; she's just up there. It's only a question of getting her down.'

'Only!' said Ginger.

They all trooped down the hill, Sim winding in the kite-string as he went. They gathered round the tree. They could see Miss Borwich, but not get to her. The first fifteen feet of the tree were without branches or even crevices to give foothold. And the bole was too big for swarming up. Johnny Bates tried getting up on Sim Tolland's shoulders to reach one of the lower branches; but that was no good. And then they heard the Park keeper behind them.

'Oy, oy, oy!' he said. 'What you playing at?'

'Our kite,' said Sim, pointing up.

'*My* kite,' said Ginger.

'Well, it'll have to stay there, won't it?' said the keeper.

'If we could borrow a long ladder,' Sim said wheedlingly; 'or even throw a rope up over a branch . . .'

'I suppose you think I'd let you go up there just to get your kite down?'

'Wouldn't you?'

'No.'

'Aaaargh!' said Sim.

'Aaaargh yourself!' said the keeper. 'And another thing: what were you up to, anyway, getting a kite snagged up in a tree in winds like these?'

This particular keeper spent most of his spare time kite-flying on Old Baldie, so he was on the side of kite-flying and kite-flyers. But his duty as a

Park keeper came first. No climbing of high trees – not for any reason at all.

Miss Borwich stayed at the top of her high tree. The Elm Street lot could see her quite clearly from Old Baldie: her coloured paper made a bright spot in the greenery. But then bad weather came, and wind and rain and even hail beat Miss Borwich about. The bright coloured paper began to rot and shred away and disappear. 'Oh, dear!' said Vera Clegg over and over again – she could hardly bear it. In the end there was only the sad skeleton of a kite perched up at the top of the tree.

Ginger Jones flatly refused to make another kite. Johnny and Kitty Bates tried making one, but – although it looked all right – it never flew well.

Sim Tolland apologized to Ginger Jones for having lost Miss Borwich; but still Ginger wouldn't make another kite.

And then came Vera Clegg's birthday. The Elm Street lot don't go in for birthday presents to each other, so they weren't paying much attention. That morning they happened to be gathered at the tree stump when Kitty Bates rushed up, hair flying, breathless. 'You've never seen such

a thing!' she cried. 'Vera's Merchant Navy uncle
has sent it to her. It's made of painted silk, black
and gold and red, and there are wings and a little
tinkly bell.'

'What are you talking about?' said Johnny.

'I'm just telling you: Vera's kite.'

Sim Tolland drew his breath in sharply. 'Come
on,' he said. He led the Elm Street lot to the
Cleggs' house, and Kitty Bates rang the bell and
asked, 'Please, can we help Vera fly her new kite?'

'Come in,' Mrs Clegg said hospitably.

They crowded into the kitchen, where Vera was
sitting at a breakfast-table covered with presents
and birthday cards from grandparents, uncles,
aunts, cousins – the Cleggs had lots of all of them.

The wastepaper-basket was overflowing with wrapping-paper and birthday card envelopes. And leaning against the wall was the kite – a huge and splendid kite, shaped like a bird, with black wings whose pinions were tipped with gold and red, and the little gilded bell of which Kitty Bates had spoken hung from what you might call its throat.

'We'll help you fly your new kite if you like, Vera,' said Sim, the first to break the silence of wonder and admiration.

'No, thank you,' Vera said faintly; and then added: 'There's no kite-string.'

'I've plenty,' said Ginger.

'No, thank you,' Vera repeated, even more faintly; but her mother said, 'You go with them, Verie. I'll just pop Jimmy into his pushchair, and he can go too. He'll be no trouble.' This was what

Mrs Clegg really thought, and Vera was such a good girl that she never contradicted.

Sim Tolland was already lifting the kite out from its place against the wall; and Ginger Jones was saying, 'I'll get my kite-string and catch you all up'; and Kitty and Johnny Bates were scrabbling in the wastepaper-basket for paper to make messengers.

All the bad feeling about losing Miss Borwich in the tree top seemed forgotten in the excitement of the wonderful new kite. Up they all went to the top of Old Baldie: Sim carrying the kite; Ginger just behind with his reel of nylon kite-string; then Kitty and Johnny; and last of all, Vera Clegg, panting behind the pushchair. She was the only one not excited, not happy.

'I'll tie the string on, Ginger,' said Sim Tolland, when they reached the top.

'Remember to knot it twice, for nylon,' said Ginger.

'Teach your grandmother . . .' said Sim. Then, calling down the slope to Vera: 'We'll just get it up for you, Vera.'

It went up like the bird it was, with a little flurry

of tinkling from its bell. A Park keeper – the kite-flying one – heard the bell from the lower slopes of Old Baldie and looked up. He saw the triumph of the bird-kite, soaring up and away.

'Here, Vera, you take it. It's your kite,' said Sim.

Vera parked the pushchair. By now the bird-kite was already small in the sky, not over their heads, but blown outwards by the wind, far beyond the limits of the Park.

Vera took the reel and held it tight and stared into the sky. She almost smiled. Kitty and Johnny Bates tore up some of their paper and began sending messengers up. Three had gone right up, when it happened. The kite-string suddenly went slack in Vera's hand; at the same time, the kite itself – as far as they could see it at that distance – began to move wildly in all directions but upwards. It seemed to have gone mad.

'The string's broken!' Kitty Bates cried.

'Couldn't,' said Ginger. 'Something's come loose. The knots – or knot.' He looked at Sim Tolland, who had tied the knots – or knot.

They watched the kite fall in mad plunges until

it disappeared from sight among the faraway houses on the other side of the Park. It was lost.

The worst was that Vera Clegg never said anything, even to Sim Tolland, whose fault it had almost certainly been. She began to cry and just cried silently on and on. She dropped the kite-string and started for home with the pushchair.

They all went home; Sim Tolland came last, by himself.

Ginger began at once to make a kite to beat all previous kites, for Vera Clegg. Sim helped him: bought anything that Ginger specially needed for the kite from his – Sim's – own pocket-money, ran the errands for him, held the gluepot when he began sticking.

When the kite was finished, Vera Clegg said: 'I don't want it.'

About a fortnight after the loss of the bird-kite, the Elm Street lot were at the tree stump, when a man in uniform turned down the street and came towards them. He was a Park keeper – *the* Park keeper. They all stared.

'Clegg of Elm Street?' the Park keeper said. He had to repeat this; and then Sim pointed to Vera and Jimmy Clegg.

'Lost anything recently?' the keeper asked.

Sim Tolland was looking at a large, flat, untidy brown paper parcel that the keeper was carrying partly behind his back. 'She's lost a kite,' Sim said. 'At least, I lost it for her.'

'What was it like?' the keeper asked Vera.

'A bird,' said Vera. 'A big, beautiful bird. It was my birthday present.'

'Ah,' said the keeper. 'Well, it came down in a garden the other side of the Park. The old grandma who found it would have given it away, but it had this messenger on it: a bit of old envelope with a name – Clegg – and what looked like the remains of an address – Elm Street. So she

gave it to someone to give to a Park keeper, and it
came to me, of course. Here you are, Clegg of Elm
Street!' He handed the parcelled-up kite to Vera.

'Thank you,' she said; and Sim Tolland and
Ginger Jones and all the rest beamed. The keeper
was pleased with himself, too.

'Tell you what,' he said heartily. 'All you lot
can come up to Old Baldie next Saturday afternoon, and I'll show Clegg of Elm Street how to
fly her own kite, and you can all watch and learn a
bit.'

'Right!' said the Elm Street lot; all except for Vera Clegg, who said, 'No, thank you.'

'But you want to fly your own kite?' said the Park keeper.

'No, thank you,' said Vera.

'But you want *someone* to fly it?'

'No, thank you,' said Vera. With her parcel in one hand and Jimmy Clegg at the end of the other, she left the stump and walked home. They watched her go.

Indoors she went straight up to her bedroom, unpacked the kite, and lovingly handled its beauty. Then she got on to a chair and hung the kite on the wall on a nail well out of Jimmy's reach. There it has stayed ever since.

The Elm Street lot say it's a pity; but it is Vera's kite. Meanwhile, they fly the other one – the kite-to-end-all-kites, that Ginger made with Sim Tolland helping. The Park keeper says it's not bad. And Sim takes his turn with the others now – not always first turn, either.

Miss Munson and the Festival of Arts, Crafts, Athletics, Pets, Gardens, and Inventions

SOME of the Elm Street lot have acquaintances –
even friends – outside Elm Street; and from time
to time these may be allowed to join in round the
tree stump.

One warmish afternoon, after school, the usual
Elm Street lot had gathered there, with others
from the next street. They had been idly tossing an
old tennis ball to and fro, and talking. The conversation turned on the differences between streets
– which was best, and why.

'No one else has a tree stump,' said Sim Tolland;
and this was true.

'There's nothing else special about Elm Street,'
said a next-street boy.

'Old Mr Crackenthorpe?' suggested Johnny Bates.

'Keep him,' said the next-street boy.

'What about Miss Munson's window-boxes?' Kitty Bates said.

The next-street lot just raised their eyebrows.

'Behind you,' said Sim, pointing to Miss Munson's very fine show of crocuses; but the next-street lot did not even bother to turn and look.

'Never gets a mention in the Festival,' said one of them. A window-box competition is part of the Woodside Festival of Arts, Crafts, Athletics, Pets, Gardens, and Inventions, which comes at the end of July.

'They're not mentioned because the Festival competition is for people with *only* window-boxes,' said Sim. 'Miss Munson has a back garden as well.'

'So there,' said Johnny Bates, who was now throwing the tennis ball rather high and catching it each time with a kind of snap.

The next-street lot then asked why Elm Street

never got a mention for Miss Munson's back garden. Sim said that Miss Munson wouldn't let anyone through the house to see it: 'But it's a prize one all right.'

'Oh, really?' said the next-street lot.

'What do you mean, "Oh, really?"' Sim asked them; and Johnny Bates was now holding his tennis ball with both hands as if it might fly off somewhere if he didn't.

'Just "Oh, really?"' said the next-street lot; and then one of them gave a nasty little laugh. And then Johnny Bates threw his tennis ball at him, hard.

Johnny meant to hit the next-street boy, but he didn't expect to; and he was right in that. The

next-street boy dodged aside, and the ball passed him, and went on – like a small express train – until it reached Miss Munson's front-room window: then, without a second's hesitation, it went through the glass and disappeared from view inside.

After the usual sound of glass breaking, there was silence. Then the whole of the next-street lot melted away from the tree stump, and Elm Street was empty of them. At the same time Johnny Bates took a sidling step towards home, but his sister caught him by one arm and Sim Tolland by the other. 'You *can't*,' they said; and, miserably, he saw that he could not.

From any other house but Miss Munson's someone would by now have come rushing out to collar Johnny Bates. Miss Munson's front door stayed shut; but a hand drew together the curtains of the broken front window.

'She's there,' said Kitty Bates, 'and she's scared.'

'She probably thinks we did it deliberately,' said Sim.

'We must explain, and Johnny must say he's

sorry,' said Kitty. She was rather enjoying herself.

The three of them knocked at Miss Munson's front door, and waited, and knocked again; but no one came. So they went into the Tollands' house, Sim leading the way, and up to Sim's bedroom. From his bedroom window they could lean out and, by looking sideways, see almost into Miss Munson's back garden. It was surrounded by high rambler-rose-grown trellises; but through the trellis-work and leaves they could just see Miss Munson standing there, facing the back of the house, apparently listening.

'Hey, Miss Munson!' Sim Tolland shouted, and Miss Munson gave a jump they could see even through the rambler-roses, and scuttled from the garden back into the shelter of the house.

'Well,' said Sim, drawing his head in again, 'we can't do more.'

Going home, Johnny and Kitty Bates had to pass Miss Munson's house again. Just as they were level with the front door, it opened for about three rattling inches. The rattling was because of the chain which Miss Munson had put across before opening: she did not intend to risk anyone's forcing an entry. Through this gap came trickling the tennis ball, fairly fast down the slight slope of the front path, under the front gate, and across the pavement almost to Johnny's feet.

'Miss Munson!' he called desperately; but her front door was shut again. He picked up the ball, and they went home.

That evening, over his tea, Mr Bates heard about the breakage. This was not the first window that Johnny had broken. So Mr Bates had a good deal to say, ending with: 'And now I suppose I shall have to go round with glass and putty and mend the old thing's window.' (All the windows of Elm Street are alike, and Mr Bates keeps putty and panes of glass by him.)

'I don't know that she'll let you in,' said

Johnny. 'Answer the door when you knock, I mean. She wouldn't for us.'

'We told you,' said Kitty.

'Not answer when I knock?' said Mr Bates. He had risen from his tea table in angry haste with his fist doubled up for knocking. Then he sat down

again. 'No, perhaps I won't. Tea first. But after tea I shall write Miss Munson a letter. I shall need a pencil and some paper and an envelope. And quiet. And then you'll push my letter under her door, Johnny-my-lad.'

What exactly Mr Bates wrote in his letter to Miss Munson is not known, but the next day when Mr Bates knocked – not loudly, but with a kind of certainty in his knocking – there was Miss Munson opening the door at once and meekly standing aside for him to come in.

Johnny and Kitty Bates went with their father: Johnny to apologize, and Kitty to help her father by holding the glass or the putty when he needed it. Of course, Johnny could have done this helping job, but his father thought that he might have enjoyed it.

This was the first time that any of the Elm Street lot had ever seen the inside of this particular house. Nobody got inside Miss Munson's house except Miss Munson and the gas-meter man.

Miss Munson had lived for years and years in Elm Street, but she had no friends or even nodding acquaintances. She went out into Elm Street only if she had to: she scurried to the shops and back as if she expected to be chased. All she cared about, people said, was her gardening.

The front room which Kitty and Johnny Bates now surveyed was bare of the usual carpeting, pictures, and furniture; but it was full of other things. There were stacks of flower-pots in one corner; there was a small lawn-mower; there was a large spade and a small spade, a large fork and a small fork and a hand fork and a trowel, a hoe, a rake, a dibber, shears, secateurs, and something that looked like the handle of a spade or fork but with a pointed, steel-shod end for making holes in the earth. On the mantelpiece old envelopes and

screws of paper contained seeds gathered from Miss Munson's own plants. Other much bigger bags and sacks, mysteriously full or partly full, lay about. The room smelt of compost.

Mr Bates looked at the bags, and also sniffed. 'Buying compost, Miss Munson?' he said. 'That comes expensive. You're a gardener: you should make your own. Potato peelings, orange skin, banana skin – anything that'll rot down – you know.' He looked at her consideringly. She was skinny: you couldn't imagine much household refuse for compost from what Miss Munson must eat. 'Ah, well,' he said, and turned to his job. 'Come on, Kitty, take this broken glass in its paper and put it into Miss Munson's dustbin.'

Kitty knew that the dustbin would be at the back, and she wanted to see the back garden properly. Johnny came too. Miss Munson followed them, making sharp twittering noises, like a bird who sees a cat nearing its nest.

All the Elm Street gardens or back yards are much the same size: if a single-decker bus lay down on its side, it would just about fit in. So there isn't all that room for lawns and arbours and shrubberies and vistas and plashing fountains and so on; but Miss Munson had got all that lot in, more or less, except for the plashing fountain. There was a little lawn and a walk, with a lavender hedge on either side, giving a vista to an arbour which would later be covered with clematis. There was a little bay tree trimmed to the shape of a toffee-apple; and one privet bush trimmed to look like a bird out of a Noah's Ark, and another to look like Noah himself.

'Oh!' said Kitty Bates in a sighing breath.

Johnny said: '*That* would show 'em. That would win a prize in the Festival! You must enter it this year, Miss Munson. You must.'

'Oh, no!' said Miss Munson. 'No, no.'

'We'll enter you,' said Kitty. 'You needn't do anything except go on gardening and then, in July, let the judges through the house to see the garden.'

'Oh, no!' said Miss Munson. 'No, no, no, no, no, no, no . . .'

By now Kitty Bates had put the broken glass into the dustbin. All that it already contained was a margarine wrapper, a tea-packet, and some smaller refuse. The compost heap, beyond the dustbin, had only garden refuse on it, and was nothing much.

'It's just a question of your getting used to the idea of the judges coming through the house to the garden,' said Johnny Bates. 'Really, it's just a question of getting used to *people*.' His eyes rested on Miss Munson's compost heap; and then he said 'Ah!' so suddenly that Miss Munson jumped, and even Kitty was surprised.

After that Johnny led the way briskly back to Mr Bates, who had just finished puttying the new pane in. He told Johnny and Kitty to take a look at how a job should be done; and he told Miss Munson she mustn't be frightened of saying boo to the Elm Street lot another time. Then the three Bateses went home; and Miss Munson thankfully shut the front door and put on the chain as usual.

But that is by no means the end of the story. The next day Johnny Bates came knocking at Miss Munson's door with a pail half-full of potato peelings, orange skin, banana skin and the rest. She opened the door on the chain, and would have shut it again when she saw who was there; but Johnny put his foot in to stop that. 'For your compost heap, Miss Munson,' said Johnny, holding the pail so that she could see inside. She looked, the tip of her nose twitched, she hesitated . . . In

the end she opened the door wide and nodded Johnny in, and he walked through the house to the compost heap in the back garden.

The next day Sim Tolland called with something for compost, and Miss Munson let him through to the garden with it. On the third day the Elm Street lot gave Miss Munson a rest. On the fourth day Vera Clegg brought her a basketful of apples that had gone rotten: Miss Munson could not resist letting her take them through to the compost heap. The next day Ginger Jones brought cabbage leaves and peelings. The next day Kitty Bates brought something. And so on and so on. Nobody brought a great deal at once; everybody insisted on taking what they brought right through the house to the garden.

So it went on; so it is still going on, for the Festival of Arts, Crafts, Athletics, Pets, Gardens, and Inventions does not take place until July. Miss Munson is having plenty of practice in *people*, and meanwhile the Elm Street lot are entering her for the Back Garden Prize. They have already told her so, and she took the news better than might have been expected.

The other afternoon the Elm Street lot were at the tree stump, and Johnny Bates had just delivered his compost to Miss Munson. He had forgotten to shut the front gate behind him, and little Jimmy Clegg – playing at being a horse as usual – had trotted in. As is the way of horses, this one began to browse on what he found: Jimmy began to pick the pansies in Miss Munson's window-boxes.

The first the Elm Street lot knew of it was a sound of rapping on glass. They turned to look, and there was Miss Munson rapping at Jimmy Clegg to stop. He didn't; so the front door opened – wide – and Miss Munson stuck her head out: 'None of that!' she said sharply, and also, 'Boo!'

Jimmy Clegg galloped off; and Johnny said with satisfaction: 'She's coming along nicely for the Festival.'